MABEL MURPLE

Sheree Fitch

Illustrations by Sydney Smith

NIMBUS
PUBLISHING

Nimbus Publishing Limited
3731 Mackintosh St, Halifax, NS B3K 5A5
(902) 455-4286 nimbus.ca

Printed and bound in Canada
Cover and interior design: Heather Bryan

Library and Archives Canada Cataloguing in Publication

Fitch, Sheree
Mabel Murple / Sheree Fitch, author ;
Sydney Smith, illustrator.
ISBN 978-1-55109-859-3 softcover
ISBN 978-1-55109-788-6 hardcover

1. Children's poetry, Canadian (English).
I. Smith, Sydney, 1980- II. Title.

PS8561.I86M32 2011   jC813'.54   C2011-903920-6

(Text previously published by Doubleday Canada Limited, 1995,
with illustrations by Maryann Kovalski)

Canadä   Canada Council   Le Conseil des Arts
          for the Arts   du Canada

NOVA SCOTIA
Communities, Culture and Heritage

Nimbus Publishing acknowledges the financial support for its publishing
activities from the Government of Canada through the Canada Book
Fund (CBF) and the Canada Council for the Arts, and from the Province
of Nova Scotia through the Department of Communities,
Culture and Heritage.

What if...

There was a purple planet
With purple people on it

Would those purple people play
Whatever purple way they wanted?

And what if...

EVERYTHING was purple
   I mean a WHOLE PURPLE WORLD
And there was someone just like me
   I mean a purple sort of girl

And if...

There was a purple girl
How purple could she be?
Would she get in purple trouble?
(She would, if she were me!)

Now...

This purple girl should have a name
What name could rhyme with purple?
I must dream up a proper name...

I'VE GOT IT!

Now that I have named her
I will dream of what she's like
Would Mabel Murple ride upon
Her purple motorbike?

(I think she might!)

Mabel Murple motored merrily
Through muddy purple puddles
She sang: "I'm a purple person!
I'll roarrrrr away my troubles!"

She wore a purple helmet
And purple leather gloves
She's the purple motorbiker
Whom everybody loves!

(What is that purple blur?
Mabel Murple—yes! It's her!)

Mabel Murple's house was purple
  So was Mabel's hair
Mabel Murple's dog was purple
  A purple poodle named Pierre

Mabel's portico was purple
  So was her bassoon
She played some purple blues
  Underneath a purple moon.

Mabel Murple had a skateboard
She skittered down the street
She wore a pair of purple sneakers
Upon her purple feet

She bumpled to a purple store
Then she slurpled purple juice
People shouted, "Skateboard Scallywag!
Mabel Murple's on the loose!"

(And they skedaddled!)

Mabel Murple ordered breakfast
She had purple eggs on toast
And when she ordered dinner
She had purple short rib roast

Mabel Murple cooked a supper
Murple's super duper purple stew
It was served with purple ketchup
And Mabel's maple syrple, too!

(Mabel Murple's purple maple syrple!)

Mabel Murple's skis were purple
She skied on purple snow
She wore a pair of purple goggles
And shouted, "Yee-haw, here I go!"

Mabel jumpled purple moguls
She slid on purple ice
Then she asked a ski instructor
For professional advice

(He said, "Sloooow down!")

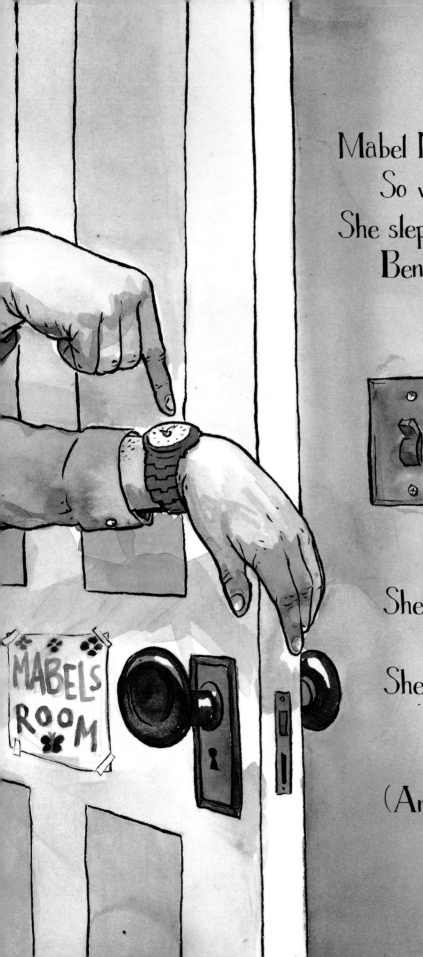

Mabel Murple's room was purple
So was Mabel's bed
She slept with purple pillows
Beneath her purple head

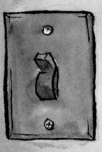

She wore purple dot pyjamas
And polka purple socks
She had a purple teddy bear
Named Snickerknickerbox!

(And he SNORED!)

Even Mabel Murple
Has to close her eyes
I wonder if she dreams
Of distant purple skies?

Perhaps she dreams of places
She has never been
Of a world with multicolours
That she has never seen

Or perhaps when Mabel Murple dreams
She dreams of...

Gertrude Green!

Gertrude Green's
house was green
So was Gertrude's hair
Gertrude Green's
cat was green
So was her...

tHe EnD